One, two, three, four,
Mary at the cottage door;
Five, six, seven, eight,
Eating cherries off a plate.

Hush-a-bye, baby, on the tree top,
When the wind blows, the cradle will rock;
When the bough breaks, the cradle will fall.
Down will come baby, cradle and all.

**The Queen of Hearts
She made some tarts,
All on a summer's day;
The Knave of Hearts,
He stole these tarts,
and took them clean away.**

To market, to market, to buy a fat pig,
Home again, home again, jiggety jig;
To market, to market, to buy a fat hog,
Home again, home again, jiggety jog.

Rub-a-dub-dub, three men in a tub,
And who do you think they be?
The butcher, the baker, the candlestick maker,
Turn them out knaves all three.

Sing a song of sixpence,
A pocket full of rye;
Four and twenty blackbirds,
Baked in a pie.
When the pie was opened
The birds began to sing;
Was not that a dainty dish
To set before a King?

The King was in his counting house,
Counting out his money;
The Queen was in the parlour
Eating bread and honey;
The maid was in the garden
Hanging out the clothes,
When down came a blackbird,
And pecked off her nose.

Polly put the kettle on
Polly put the kettle on
Polly put the kettle on
We'll all have tea.
Sukey take it off again
Sukey take it off again
Sukey take it off again
They've all gone away.

Ride a cock horse to Banbury Cross,
To see a fine lady upon a white horse;
Rings on her fingers and bells on her toes,
She shall have music wherever she goes.

Baa, baa, black sheep, have you any wool?
Yes sir, yes sir, three bags full;
One for the master, and one for the dame,
And one for the little boy
Who lives down the lane.

Old Mother Hubbard
Went to the cupboard
To get her poor dog a bone;
But when she got there
The cupboard was bare,
And so the poor dog had none.

She went to the baker's
To buy him some bread;
But when she came back
The poor dog was dead.

She went to the joiner's
To buy him a coffin;
But when she came back
The poor dog was laughing.

She took a clean dish
To get him some tripe;
But when she came back
He was smoking a pipe.

She went to the ale-house
To get him some beer;
But when she came back
The dog sat in a chair.

She went to the seamstress
To buy him some linen;
But when she came back
The dog was spinning.

She went to the fruiterer's
To buy him some fruit;
But when she came back
He was playing the flute.

She went to the cobbler's
To buy him some shoes;
But when she came back
He was reading the news.

She went to the tavern
For white wine and red;
But when she came back
The dog stood on his head.

She went to the hosier's
To buy him some hose;
But when she came back
He was dressed in his clothes.

The dame made a curtsey,
The dog made a bow;
The dame said, 'Your servant.'
The dog said, 'Bow-wow.'

Cock-a-doodle-doo!
My dame has lost her shoe,
My master's lost his fiddling stick,
And doesn't know what to do.

It's raining, it's pouring,
The old man is snoring;
He went to bed
And bumped his head,
And couldn't get up in the morning.

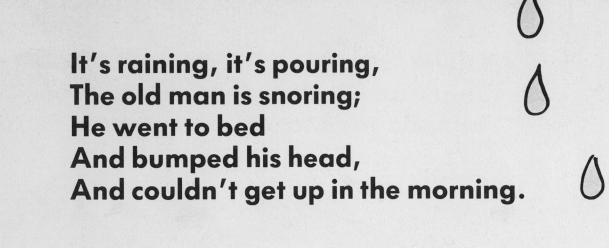

A dillor, a dollar, a ten o'clock scholar
What makes you come so soon?
You used to come at ten o'clock,
But now you come at noon.

Ding, dong, bell,
Pussy's in the well.
Who put her in?
Little Johnny Green.
Who pulled her out?
Little Johnny Stout.
Oh, what a naughty boy was that,
To try and drown poor pussy cat,
Who never did him any harm,
But kill all the mice in the farmer's barn.

Twinkle, twinkle little star,
How I wonder what you are
Up above the world so high,
Like a diamond in the sky.